Glamour and excitement!

↑ stardom! ↗

✳ Fame and fortune ✳
could be one step away!

Welcome to

Fame School

For another fix of

read

Fame School

Dancing Star

For everyone in M&L Productions
They made me who I am today

First published in 2008 by Usborne Publishing Ltd., Usborne House,
83-85 Saffron Hill, London EC1N 8RT, England. www.usborne.com

A CIP catalogue record for this book is available from the British Library.

JFMAMJJA OND/08

ISBN 9780746097168

Printed in Great Britain.

1 Some Exciting News

"Marmalade?"

Marmalade wasn't paying attention. He quite often had problems concentrating, and just now he was miles away. The five other students in the dance class had been paying close attention to what their teacher was saying, but Marmalade was thinking about how funny his biology teacher had looked when she'd walked into assembly that morning. It was something to do with the way she rolled her feet a bit sideways as she moved her weight from one foot to the other. Marmalade was well known for his mimicry, and he couldn't resist thinking about trying this walk. He knew it would make his classmates laugh if he could get it right…

"Marmalade!"

He jumped as Mr. Penardos shouted at him. "Sorry. I didn't hear what you were saying," Marmalade apologized quickly. But his dance teacher wasn't fooled.

"You didn' hear because you weren' listening," complained Mr. Penardos crossly. "I think perhaps I won' tell you, and you will miss out on this exciting chance."

"What chance?" Marmalade was paying attention now! "Do you think I'm in with a chance of being the next prom king?"

Mr. Penardos smiled. He never stayed cross for long, and he liked Marmalade Stamp. In spite of his periodic daydreaming, and the fact that he was the class clown, Marmalade was a very rewarding dancer to teach.

"I don' know about that," he said. "I was telling the class about the scout that is coming tomorrow."

"Scout? What for?" asked Marmalade. His friend and fellow dancer, Jack, groaned.

"It's a company called M&L Productions. They're casting a new pop video, and are looking for dancers,"

Jack explained. "We've already been through all this while you were staring out of the window."

"Sorry," said Marmalade again, excitement rippling through his mind. "That *is* good news. Who's the singer?"

"I don' have any news about the singer yet," said Mr. Penardos. "The production company is keeping the name secret at the moment."

"Why would they do that?" asked Jack in a puzzled voice.

"They might want to have a big build-up and launch for the video," suggested Mr. Penardos. "And if details got out too soon it could ruin the effect. These days, spoiler articles can get put out so quickly on the internet. There's no point in having a big launch if everyone already knows what you're doing."

"Wouldn't it be brilliant to get chosen?" said Marmalade. "I'd love to be in on a big secret. I wouldn't give it away, however much the media tried to bribe me."

"You're such a dreamer you probably wouldn't remember who it was even if you *did* get offered a bribe," said Martin, another dancer in the class.

Everyone laughed, including Marmalade. He didn't mind being teased, especially as Martin was probably right. By now, it was the end of the lesson. Marmalade picked up his towel, slung it round his neck and said goodbye to the girls. Ellie, Megan and Alice were heading off to their boarding house to shower and get changed, and the boys needed to do the same.

"See you at tea," he said to Alice.

"If you remember to turn up for it," she joked, as she headed out of the door.

There was some free time before tea, and the boys chatted after they'd showered. "Are you going to go for this video job if we get the chance?" Marmalade asked the others. He paused outside the room he shared with Danny, Ed and Ben.

"Of course!" said Jack, and Martin nodded his agreement.

"We'd be daft not to," said Martin, leaning against the doorpost. "Think about it. We'd earn money! These jobs can pay quite well."

Marmalade and Jack laughed. It was Martin's dream to buy a Porsche once he was eighteen, but he had a very long way to go before he'd have saved anything like enough money to do that!

"So you just want to do it for the car fund," teased Marmalade. "Have you got enough to buy a wing mirror yet?"

"You wait," said Martin. "If you get into the pop video circuit it's brilliant. My uncle told me. One job can lead to another and before you know it…yellow Porsche, leather seats, everything! And my uncle says the experience is really good too," he added. "You can meet some important people."

Martin's uncle was currently in America appearing in a show on Broadway; he'd danced in several cool films as well. It was hard, making a living as a dancer, so the small number of dance students in Martin's year hung on his every word when he spoke about his uncle.

"Well I'm up for it," said Marmalade. "It sounds great."

"Me too," said Jack. "We need to take every chance we get in this business."

"So what's the best way to prepare?" asked Marmalade.

Martin grinned. "I'm not telling you that! It's every man for himself as far as this job is concerned!" He stopped leaning on the doorpost and sauntered into his room.

Marmalade sighed. "I can't blame him," he said to Jack. "If I had any hot tips I'd keep them to myself at a time like this. Did Mr. Penardos say anything about preparation?"

"Nothing specific," said Jack. "He said the production company haven't told the school exactly what they're looking for, but that quality always counts. He also said we need to keep developing our stamina, because filming can be exhausting."

"So we need to be good at everything, I suppose," said Marmalade. "That's not much help, is it?"

"Well, I think he just meant that we ought to be ourselves," Jack said. "And let our ability and style show. There's nothing else we *can* do. Anyway, see you later."

Some Exciting News

Marmalade watched as Jack walked elegantly down the corridor to the room he shared with Ravi and two other boys.

Jack stood out amongst Marmalade's dancing friends because of his small stature and natural grace. He'd had a lot of ballet training before he came to Rockley Park School, and it showed. Next to Jack, Marmalade always felt rather lacking in poise, especially since he'd got a lot taller recently. He knew he was one of the finest dancers in the class, but all the same, he was beginning to feel a bit awkward now he was growing so fast. He'd thought he'd got over being self-conscious of the way he looked – in fact he'd played up to it in the past – but at the moment he wasn't so sure of himself.

It was all very well Mr. Penardos saying that quality counted. But if the scout was taken by Jack's grace, or Martin's suppleness, he might not notice Marmalade's excellent balance and fantastic jumps.

Marmalade went into his room and closed the door. He was alone, because the other boys were over in the Rock Department finishing off their lessons. He glanced at himself in the mirror. He definitely needed an edge. He needed something extra to make sure the scout noticed him as a superb dancer, not a boy growing so fast that his arms and legs seemed to be too long for the rest of his body.

He thought hard for a moment and then a smile crept across his face. He knew exactly who to ask for help. He was sure she could boost his self-confidence and give him the edge he wanted. Marmalade shook his damp hair into place. He'd go and find her now. With her knowledge and help, he was sure he'd make quite an impact!

2 Pop to the Rescue

"But your hair is your best bit!" Pop Lowther and her twin sister Lolly were standing outside the singing teacher's room. Pop had crossed her arms, and was frowning at Marmalade. The twins were models as well as singers, and they knew all about the importance of image. Marmalade had been sure that Pop would help him out, but she didn't seem to be on his wavelength.

"Come on, Pop," said Marmalade. "I came to you because I thought you'd help me. You must have some ideas. I really want to stand out!"

Pop giggled. "You *do* stand out," she said. "In the nicest possible way – with your amazing hair and your big grin. Who could miss you?"

Marmalade sighed. "I'm just worried about how I look now I've grown so much," he said. "I can't see that any scout would choose me over any of the others."

"Don't write yourself off before the scout has even come!" said Pop.

"You must be able to think of *something* I can do to make them notice me," insisted Marmalade.

Pop looked hard at him. "You want to make the best of what you've got," she told him.

"What *have* I got?" he asked worriedly.

"You've got this amazing hair, great height, and a huge personality," Lolly told him. "Why not wear something extrovert to complement those things?"

"I don't have any very interesting dance clothes," Marmalade told her. "No one has. Loose trousers and sweaty T-shirts aren't exactly exciting, are they?"

"Well then, why don't you add something to them to make you stand out?" suggested Lolly thoughtfully. "Like a headband...or..." She trailed off as she continued to think.

"I know!" said Pop. "Your best thing is the way you can jump and spin, isn't it?"

"Ye-es," he agreed. "Why?"

"Well, you need something flowing that will look good when you're leaping through the air," she said. "You don't want a normal headband, you want something more like a long silk scarf."

"That's right!" agreed Lolly. "Why not go for something like a gypsy look? Scarves are the way to go. Tie a silk scarf round your head, and another round your neck..."

"And tie one round each arm too, just above your elbow," said Pop. "That would be good. When you do those fantastic leaps of yours they'll fly out and look really cool. There you are," she told him, with a grin. "You'll be a wild, gypsy dancer. Go for it!"

Marmalade nodded, looking a lot happier. "I love that idea," he said. "I'm never going to be another Jack, am I? And you're right. I should focus on what I do best." Then he frowned. "But the scout is coming tomorrow. Do you have any scarves I could borrow?"

"Of course!" said Pop. "We've got loads, haven't we, Lolly?"

Lolly smiled. "We certainly have," she agreed.

Marmalade did a quick spin, grinning all over his face. "Can we go and sort something out now?" he asked. "Before tea?"

"Come on then," said Pop. "The scarves are in our bedroom. We can see what will work best at the house."

The three friends hurried over to the girls' boarding house. As soon as they got there, they left Marmalade in the common room and dashed off to search their bedroom. Marmalade joined Chloe, who was playing a computer game.

"Hello!" she said. "What brings you over here? We don't often see you in our house."

Marmalade explained. Chloe thought he'd make a great gypsy, and as soon as the twins came back with their arms full of scarves, she pounced on a beautiful, bright green one.

"You ought to tie that one round your head," she told him. "It'll look fantastic with your ginger hair."

"Cool!" said Marmalade, putting it on straight away.

Pop giggled. "You look very striking," she told him. "Maybe that's all you need."

"No way!" he insisted. "I want to look like a raggedy, exotic, gypsy dancer." Marmalade shook his head and the green chiffon billowed out behind him.

"Okay then," said Pop, taking charge. "How about blue for round your neck?" She took a square of electric-blue silk and tied it at a jaunty angle.

"There are two of these long, multicoloured ones," said Lolly. "Would you like them for your arms?"

"Let's try it."

"Well!" said Chloe hesitantly, when they were on. "You look a bit odd standing still, but give us a twirl, Marmalade. Let's see what you look like when you move."

He did a quick pirouette and the girls all clapped. The effect was fantastic. As he twirled around, the light fabric on his head and arms streamed out, following his movements.

"That's better," said Chloe. "You're just like my idea

of a bold, gypsy dancer now. You look brilliant! It's a pity you don't have any gold earrings, though."

"I've got a pair," said Pop, but Marmalade shook his head.

"No way!" he told them. "Scarves are fine, but I can do without the jewellery. Anyway, I've never fancied having my ears pierced." Everyone laughed at his stubborn expression.

"It's all right," smiled Lolly. "You look great just as you are."

"Please don't tell anyone what we've been doing," begged Marmalade. "It'll be good if I can keep it a surprise. Otherwise the others will start coming up with ideas too and I'll lose the advantage."

"Okay," the girls agreed. "Good luck tomorrow!"

The next morning the dance students were very excited. Marmalade usually got changed in his room, and walked over to the main school building, where the class was held, but today he got changed in a loo near the dance studio. It was quite tricky tying the scarves round his upper arms by himself and he was anxious not to be late. He quickly added the green scarf around his long, ginger curls, then opened the door of the studio. He was the last to arrive, and everyone stared at him.

"What's the bandana for?" said Martin. "You don't usually wear one."

"The scout's here!" hissed Jack. "Had you forgotten?"

"It's not fancy dress!" said Ellie, another member of the class.

Marmalade scowled at her. "Of course I haven't forgotten about the scout," he told Jack. "I'm wearing this on purpose."

Jack looked puzzled. "But why?"

"Wait and see," said Marmalade, anxiously hoping the others would be impressed once he started dancing.

"I *like* the bandana," said Alice. "The colour is great with your red hair."

"Thanks!" said Marmalade. At least *she* didn't thing he looked totally stupid.

Dancing Star

There was no time to say any more because Mr. Penardos clapped his hands to get their attention. "Today we welcome Mrs. Dreyfus to our lesson," he said. "She would like you all to act as if she isn' here while you warm up and go through what we've been doing this term. At the end she may ask someone to remain behind. If she does, would the rest of you please go on to your nex' lesson and tell the teacher some of you may be a little late?"

Everyone nodded, but Marmalade knew that each student desperately hoped that they would be kept behind to meet the scout! He *had* to get chosen! He simply *had* to. It would be awful to have to slink off to geography, knowing that he hadn't been picked.

Mrs. Dreyfus was a small, bird-like woman. She sat quietly at the back of the room while the students warmed up and Mr. Penardos began the class.

Everyone was trying to ignore her, and most students managed quite well, but Marmalade found it impossible. Mr. Penardos had already raised his eyebrows at Marmalade's unusual attire, and

Marmalade was a bit worried he'd made a big mistake.

But he felt better once he was able to show off his particular skills. Mr. Penardos put some music on and the students began the "free expression" part of the class. Marmalade indulged in some fine jumps and a prolonged spin. The scarves really came into their own then. He could see the other students pausing to watch him and hoped that Mrs. Dreyfus was doing so, too. He stopped spinning and glanced over towards her. But he should have made sure of his balance first. Instead of stopping perfectly after the spin he staggered slightly. He bit his lip in annoyance. He felt so stupid! He told himself to take more care, and for the rest of the class he made sure his moves were flawless.

Mr. Penardos and Mrs. Dreyfus were deep in conversation at the end of the class, but the students couldn't hear what they were saying.

"I hate waiting," said Jack to Marmalade. "Why can't she put us out of our misery and let us know what she's decided?"

"Here they come," muttered Martin.

Mr. Penardos clapped his hands, and everyone fell silent.

"I woul' like to ask these people to stay behind," said Mr. Penardos. "Martin Kwame."

Martin raised his arms in triumph and a grin spread over his face.

"Ellie Edwards."

Ellie turned pink and did a small jump. She beamed at Marmalade and he summoned a weak smile for her.

"And Marmaduke Stamp."

Marmalade hated his proper name, but he was thrilled to hear it now.

"Yes!" He grinned at Martin and Ellie. It was fantastic to have been chosen. No more names were called out, and Marmalade went straight over to Jack to commiserate. "I'm really sorry you didn't get picked," he told his friend. "I wish we could be in the video together."

"Oh well," said Jack, looking dejected in spite of his words. "Maybe I'll get another chance in the future."

"I'm sure you will," agreed Marmalade, clapping him

on the back. He was trying to be sympathetic, but it was hard to hide his own delight.

"So you three please stay behind," said Mr. Penardos. "An' the other three can go."

Marmalade tried to control his breathing, but his heart was thumping with excitement. He should be going off for a shower and then to geography, but instead Mrs. Dreyfus was coming over to him. What would she want her chosen dancers to do next?

3 A Bit of a Shock

Mr. Penardos introduced Marmalade and the others to Mrs. Dreyfus. She shook their hands and smiled at them all.

"I'm very pleased to have found three possible dancers for the video," she said.

Marmalade frowned, but Ellie spoke first. "*Possible* dancers?" she said. "I thought you'd chosen us?"

Mrs. Dreyfus shook her head. "It's not just down to me," she said. "I vet all the dancers first, but then they have to be approved by the singer, as well as the choreographer, director...a whole collection of people."

Ellie looked embarrassed. "Of course," she agreed. "Sorry. I got carried away with the excitement of being picked. So does that mean we get to dance in front of whoever the singer is?" she asked.

Mrs. Dreyfus laughed. "No," she said. "I take your photograph, and the decisions are made that way."

"So we get chosen from a picture?" Marmalade was outraged. He'd put so much thought and effort into this trial, and in the end it came down to a snapshot!

"It is very important for this video that every young dancer we have is talented," Mrs. Dreyfus explained. "I wouldn't just take anyone off the street. That is why I've come here, to Rockley Park. You are all very gifted dancers, and about the right age and size too. You three have done really well to get through to this round of the selection. But it's entirely possible that *none* of you will appear in the video. We have so many people to choose between, and we've already decided on at least half the dancers. We use people we've worked with before whenever possible, you understand. So..." Mrs. Dreyfus held up her hand and, for the first time, Marmalade noticed the small camera she was holding. "I will take your pictures, put my notes about you onto the back of each photograph, and they will be entered into the final selection for discussion."

First, she photographed Ellie. She took close-ups, and full-length pictures too, but she wasn't interested in any particular dance poses. She did the same with Martin and then she turned to Marmalade.

Marmalade didn't know whether or not it would be best to smile, and Mrs. Dreyfus hadn't given them any clues. He decided that maybe it was better to look like the sort of person who would take the job seriously, so he put on what he hoped was a very responsible, grown-up expression for the close-ups. After Mrs. Dreyfus had taken all the pictures she started to put her camera away and then changed her mind.

"Do me a pirouette," she said to Marmalade. "And try not to look quite so miserable!"

Marmalade felt rather insulted that his purposeful expression had been misinterpreted as misery. But if Mrs. Dreyfus wanted a smile she could have one! He held himself ready and took a deep breath. As he pirouetted, the scarves flew out and turned his top half into a spinning mass of colour. It was so exhilarating, the huge smile on his face came really easily.

Mrs. Dreyfus put her camera away and shook hands with Mr. Penardos. She nodded to the dancers. "You'll hear in a week or so," she told them. "Good luck!"

"I'll see you to your car," said Mr. Penardos. "Off you go now, you three," he added to the students. "And please give my apologies to your teacher. You've missed rather more of your next lesson than I had anticipated."

"Well!" said Ellie, once the adults had gone. "I can't believe we've got to wait a whole week. I'm not sure I can stand the suspense!"

"At least we're in with a chance," said Martin. "My uncle told me that decisions are often down to more than one person, so I'm not surprised we have to wait."

"And you got an extra picture taken," Ellie said to Marmalade. "That's got to be good news for you."

Marmalade shrugged. In spite of being one of the three selected dancers he felt a bit disheartened. It was such a shame they would have to wait for a final decision. "Maybe they'll have a good laugh at my

Dancing Star

pirouette picture," he muttered. "They'll be looking at it and saying, *This one's obviously desperate for the part – look at what he's wearing!*"

"I'm sure they wouldn't be so horrible," said Ellie. "It was only a few scarves, and you looked fantastic during the pirouette. Anyway, I'm off for a quick shower. I can't turn up for geography all sweaty."

"Me too," agreed Martin. "Coming, Marmalade?"

Although they hurried they were all late for geography, but the teacher was very understanding. Pop shot Marmalade a questioning glance, and Marmalade knew that she and everyone else would be dying to find out how they'd all got on.

"Are you in the video?"

"What was the scout like?"

"Do you know who the singer is?"

"Where's it going to be filmed?"

As soon as the lesson was over Marmalade, Martin and Ellie were bombarded with questions.

"We don't know much about it yet," said Martin.

Ellie told them about Marmalade's photograph.

A Bit of a Shock

"I think it's good news," Pop told him. "And I'm sure she wouldn't have taken it if we hadn't made an effort with your look."

The next few days were pretty tedious as far as Marmalade was concerned. There was no news from Mrs. Dreyfus, and schoolwork was piling up. There would be school exams soon, and everyone was expected to have done loads of revision already. Marmalade found normal lessons pretty boring, and any thought of having to do extra work appalled him. He wasn't making much of an effort, and his teachers were annoyed.

"Exams are important," said Mrs. Pinto, in biology one day. "You won't do well in your GCSEs in the future if you don't practise exam technique. And you won't have a hope of passing these school exams if you don't know the work!" She gave Marmalade and Pop each a hard stare. They were the worst in the class when it came to anything academic.

At lunchtime Pop and Marmalade sat together in the dining room so they could have a good moan.

"Revision's so boring!" complained Marmalade. "All Danny wants to do is catch up after he was off with flu, and Ed and Ben are doing loads of work as well."

"Chloe and Lolly are at it all the time too," Pop said. "Tara is the only one who doesn't seem worried by exams. But then she finds everything so easy she doesn't need to."

"Lucky her!" said Marmalade gloomily.

"Stop moping," said Pop, who could never stay down for long. "Let's talk about something more interesting."

"Like what?" asked Marmalade. "The only thing I can think about is the video, but I probably haven't been picked."

Pop poked Marmalade in the ribs. "You said you were going to put that out of your mind," she told him. "Now listen. The notice has gone up today about the Lower School Prom. Our year has to organize it this time."

Marmalade groaned. "I love parties when I can just turn up and enjoy them," he complained. "I don't want to have to organize one! I just want to be prom king."

A Bit of a Shock

"Well you'll have to be a *bit* organized if you want to be prom king," Pop told him. "You'll need to sign up to say you want to do it, and you ought to make a poster or something so people will know to vote for you. I'm going to make lots of posters asking people to vote for me to be the queen." She gave Marmalade a sideways look. "You'll only get the votes in if you make an effort, and you know it," she said. "But if we organize the prom we can make lots of important decisions."

"Like what sort of food and drink to have – and the music."

"And what the theme should be, if we have one," said Pop.

"I can't remember what the theme was last year," said Marmalade, getting interested in spite of himself.

"That's because there wasn't one," Pop told him. "It was just a dance: a very nice one, but *we* can do better! With a bit of work we could make it really special."

"How about a street theme?" suggested Marmalade, already seeing himself as the centre of attention. "With graffiti decorations? I *love* street dancing."

"Er…maybe not," said Pop, looking deeply unimpressed. "But let's give it time and we'll come up with something brilliant. We'll need a group of us to do it. It'll be fun!"

"Hmm. I *like* the idea of being in charge," said Marmalade. "If we get it right, this year's prom could go down in Rockley Park history!"

"I've got a great dress to wear," said Pop dreamily. "We'll have to choose some really special music for the dancing." She leaned her head on his shoulder and gazed up at him. "Will you be my beau at the ball?" she asked in a silly voice.

Marmalade grinned. "Possibly," he told her. "You're a good dancer. And I only dance with the best."

"Honestly!" she said, sounding miffed. "You can be so pompous sometimes." But then her mouth creased into a smile and she couldn't help laughing.

"Thanks, Pop," he said, giving her a brief hug. "You've really cheered me up. I've got something to look forward to now – and it's got nothing to do with being in a pop video. Let's see if we can get an organizing committee going, and make this the best prom ever!"

4 Busy, Busy, Busy!

As the days passed, Marmalade didn't have much time to fret about the video. In between teachers piling more and more work on them, he and Pop kept talking about the prom. It seemed no one else was anxious to start things happening until after the exams were over, but Pop didn't think that was soon enough.

"We should at least decide who's going to do what," she insisted one lunchtime. "If we can just get a committee together we'll be ready to start work as soon as the exams have finished."

Committees and meetings were usually a huge turn-off for Marmalade, but this time he had his own thoughts on the matter.

Busy, Busy, Busy!

"If we're not careful the girls will take over and decide everything," he told his best friend, Danny, one afternoon when they were revising in their room.

"Well make sure you're on the committee then," said Danny. "And why don't you put a notice up asking for volunteers right away? You and Pop could put your names at the top."

"You could sign up too," urged Marmalade.

"I'm too far behind in my work to think about anything else at the moment," said Danny.

Marmalade sighed. Exams spoiled everything. "At least they've given us a bit of time to revise out of class," he said, twiddling a pencil. "Doing revision in class is grim."

Danny looked up from his history book. "Only because you mess about and get told off by the teachers," he said. "It's going to get grim in here too if you don't let me get on," he added.

"So-rry!" said Marmalade in an injured voice. There was silence for a few moments, but he couldn't stay quiet for long. "What are you revising now?" he asked.

"Okay. Okay!" he said, seeing that Danny really was fed up with him. "I'll do some work too. I promise!"

He got his history book out and sighed. At least it wasn't maths!

For a while there was silence in the room. To his surprise, Marmalade was getting quite interested in what he was reading. It was all about the Battle of Britain. The Spitfire pilots seemed very heroic. He made a few notes, and turned another page. *Some* history was like reading a story, when it was well told.

They'd been working for about half an hour when Ed arrived from the homework room, where he'd been studying with Ben. "There's a message for you from Mr. Penardos," he told Marmalade. "He wants to see you just before tea."

Marmalade pulled his phone out of his pocket and looked at the time. "It'll be about the video," he said, trying not to get excited – and failing. "Tea is in twenty minutes, so I might as well go now." Maybe he'd been chosen, and would be whisked away from revision to start learning the dance right away? "I'll do some more revision later," he said to Danny, throwing the book onto his bed.

Danny looked at him and rolled his eyes. "Yeah. Right," he said. "I'll believe it when I see it!"

Marmalade ran downstairs and out of the house. He should have carried on working until teatime, but he couldn't possibly have concentrated, knowing that Mr. Penardos wanted to see him. Had he already seen Ellie and Martin, or was Marmalade the first?

It only took a couple of minutes to race over to the main house. Marmalade went to the staffroom and knocked on the door.

"He's not here," said Mr. Clark, a maths teacher. "Hang on. I'll have a look at his timetable." Marmalade waited impatiently. "He's got a lesson," Mr. Clark told Marmalade. "So he'll be tied up until just before tea. Come back in a quarter of an hour and I expect you'll catch him then."

"Thanks." Marmalade turned away. He didn't want to hang about, but he couldn't interrupt a lesson, however much he wanted to. He would just have to wait. But Marmalade was much too jittery to sit quietly outside the staffroom. Instead he went outside, where the sun was shining. He found a shady spot and did a few stretches. Then he started jogging around thelake. Dancers needed to be fit, and he'd find it easier to wait if he was on the move. Once he'd done that it was nearly time for Mr. Penardos's lesson to end, so Marmalade made his way anxiously to the dance studio, so he could catch his teacher as he came out.

Sure enough, it wasn't long before a few senior dancers emerged from their class, chatting away happily. As soon as they'd gone, Marmalade went into the studio. Mr. Penardos was there.

"Hello, Marmalade!" said Mr. Penardos. "You came very quickly. My class is only jus' finished."

"Is it about the video?" asked Marmalade straight away. He couldn't bear to wait any longer.

Mr. Penardos smiled. "Yes," he said. "An' it is good news for you. They would like you to join them for a rehearsal next week. You're in!"

Marmalade's face split into a wide grin. "Really? Fantastic!"

"I thought you'd be pleased," said Mr. Penardos.

"What about the other two?" asked Marmalade quickly.

Mr. Penardos looked serious.

"They haven't got in, have they?" said Marmalade, sadly. He could tell from the way Mr. Penardos looked that it was bad news.

The teacher shook his head. "Unfortunately not," he said. "I saw them earlier on, before the last lesson. They were disappointed, of course."

"I bet." Marmalade felt very sorry for them. It would have been great to go to rehearsals with a couple of friends. And of course they'd be gutted. But however sorry Marmalade was, he couldn't help being thrilled for himself. He tried to stop his mind running on ahead, with visions of fame and fortune, while Mr. Penardos was still speaking.

"It's a great pity for them," he said. "Bu' it's jus' the way it goes sometimes."

"Yes," agreed Marmalade. "Do you know who the singer is yet?"

Mr. Penardos shook his head. "They're still being very secretive about tha'," he said. "You might not find out until the video shoot."

"Well thanks for the news," said Marmalade. It was still sinking in, but he felt a huge bubble of excitement threatening to burst out at any minute. He had to get away and let off steam. And he needed to tell people. Anyone would do!

He left the dance studio and rushed to the dining room. Danny, Ed and Ben were there already, as well as some of the girls in his class. He felt like doing a huge leap to get their attention, but he'd made the mistake of doing that in the dining room before, and didn't want to get injured again. Instead he threw his arms wide and yelled.

"I've done it! I've got in!"

Their reaction was a little disappointing. Loads of people turned to look at him for a few seconds and grinned, but then turned away again. Marmalade ignored the older students. He knew they wouldn't be interested, but his classmates ought to be happy for him. He went up to the table where Danny was sitting and tried again.

"Be happy!" he said. "Smile! I've been chosen to dance in the video. Isn't that cool?"

"Great," smiled Danny. "Congratulations."

Only then did Marmalade notice that Martin and Ellie were sitting nearby.

"Hey, I'm so sorry you didn't get in," he told them. "It would've been really cool to work on the video together. Better luck next time, eh?"

"Yeah, well. Congratulations to you anyway," said Ellie.

"Respect," said Martin, gently punching Marmalade's fist.

"Thanks," said Marmalade, and he went to the serving hatch to get some tea. He joined Danny at his table.

"Any plans for this evening?" he asked his friend.

"More revision," Danny told him. "It's the first exam in the morning and I want to look over some history dates."

Dancing Star

"Oh come on!" said Marmalade. "I've just had some good news. I want to celebrate!"

Danny gave Marmalade an understanding smile. "We will celebrate," he promised. "But not tonight. Honestly, Marmalade, we need to do our best for these exams or we'll be in big trouble. Let's wait until after they're over."

Marmalade pushed his salad round his plate grumpily. He wanted to celebrate *now*! He might not feel like it in five days' time. He looked around. Everyone seemed to be obsessed by exams. He swallowed his food hurriedly and stacked his plate.

"Where are you going?" asked Danny.

"To find someone who *does* want to celebrate," he said, standing up. "I *know* I should be sensible and wait, but I can't help it. I need to celebrate *now*!"

 5 Friends

Marmalade didn't have a clue what he was going to do. After all, *he* ought to be thinking about exams as well. He knew Danny was right. But everyone was so serious about it. Why couldn't they just lighten up a bit?

He was so busy complaining to himself that he wasn't looking where he was walking, and bumped right into Pop.

"Whoops! Sorry!" he said, catching her arm. "I didn't see you there."

"I wasn't exactly hiding!" she told him. "You weren't looking."

Marmalade told her his news and at last he got the response he'd been hoping for.

"Wow! That's fantastic!" Pop yelled. "Well done! I bet those scarves helped!"

"Well, maybe," he said, disentangling himself from the huge hug she was giving him. "Thanks!"

"And your talent," she added enthusiastically. "We mustn't forget that. Talent is the most important thing of all. No wonder you got a place. You are *such* a brilliant dancer."

"Well, I hope I'll do all right," said Marmalade, trying to sound vaguely modest. It was great having Pop around. She was such fun to be with.

She gave him another hug and he hugged her back. "Anyway, where were you off to in such a rush?" she asked, releasing him with a giggle.

"Oh. I was just hoping for some reaction to my good news, back there in the dining room," he explained. "But everyone is so obsessed with exams, and I got fed up." He hesitated. "I know I ought to be working too, but I hate revision."

"Me too," said Pop. "But I've got a strategy this year."

"What is it?" said Marmalade. "Come on, you can tell me."

"Well, I decided that the only way I was going to make myself sit and revise for an hour was to break it up into manageable bits," she said. "And I can only do that if I reward myself each time I've done…say fifteen minutes of work."

"So how do you reward yourself?" said Marmalade.

Pop giggled. "With these!" She pulled a large tube of sweets out of her pocket. "I don't usually eat sweets," she explained. "But this is an emergency! I only thought of it a couple of days ago, but it really works for me."

"That's a great idea!" said Marmalade. "I wish I'd thought of it. But it's almost too late now. Exams start tomorrow."

"It's never too late!" said Pop. "In fact I was going to go and do some revision now. Do you fancy sharing? We could test each other for tomorrow's exam, and award sweets for excellence!"

"Okay," said Marmalade. "Let's do it!"

The sweets didn't exactly make the revision any

easier, but they did help things along, and having Pop with him was fantastic. It was so good to be with someone who felt the same way he did. Together they rattled through loads of work, and although they didn't expect to do very well in the exams, at least they felt they'd made an effort.

The next morning they went into the exam room together. Their desks were miles apart, but just before they turned over their pages Marmalade gave Pop a huge wink. She giggled and winked back. Marmalade grinned. If they had to do these stupid exams it was far better to have a bit of a laugh as well.

The exams lasted for the whole week, and over those few days, Pop and Marmalade became inseparable, so much so that they came in for some teasing from their friends.

"Pop's in love!" said Tara one morning, as Pop sped off to sit with Marmalade at breakfast. Pop stuck her tongue out at Tara.

But neither Pop nor Marmalade minded being teased. They were having fun – and getting through some work. And, when they weren't in the throes of exams, they were speculating about the video or discussing the Lower School Prom. Several other students had agreed to help, but it seemed that most of them were happy to let Pop and Marmalade do all the work, so they needed to share out the jobs that would have to be done.

"We've almost got enough people on the organizing committee now," Pop told Marmalade one afternoon.

"There are too many girls, though," Marmalade said, looking through the list.

"Well, if you could find a couple more boys that would be great," she agreed. "We still need someone to sort out tables and chairs. We won't want them set out in the usual dining-room pattern, will we? That would be too canteen-like."

"Well it *is* a canteen, stupid," Marmalade said with a smile.

Pop shoved his arm. "You know what I mean," she said. "Stop trying to wind me up." They looked at each other and grinned.

Dancing Star

The following week, Marmalade had his first video rehearsal. Mrs. Player took him. She often acted as a "minder" for the students. The rehearsal room was in a scruffy old building in the nearby city. It didn't look much from the outside. Inside, though, there were several practice rooms with sprung floors and full-length mirrors. Mrs. Player delivered Marmalade to the right room, then went to wait in a small café area in the basement.

It was very exciting to be there, but Marmalade felt nervous on his own. He wished Martin or Ellie could have been with him. There were about twenty dancers in the room, and it seemed quite a few of them knew each other. Several of them glanced at him as he came in, but no one came over to say hello. Marmalade wasn't usually shy, but he couldn't help feeling a bit intimidated. He was determined not to show it, though, so he headed straight for a small group and introduced himself.

"Hi!" he said. "I'm Marmalade. I don't know anyone here."

It did the trick. At once people started to introduce themselves to him. As soon as they realized that this was his first proper job they couldn't have been more helpful.

"We're just waiting for things to kick off," explained Paz.

"We don't know what we're expected to do yet," chipped in Kerry.

"I expect the dance director will be here soon," said Nina.

"Cool hair!" said Neil. "Is it naturally curly?"

Marmalade nodded. Looking around, he realized that all the dancers had quite long, wild hair. And they were all as lanky as him. It occurred to him that Martin, with his excellent physique, and Ellie, with her close-cropped hair, wouldn't have looked right in this group.

After a few minutes the door opened and three women and a man came in. "Hi there!" said the man, who had a short, grey beard and twinkling eyes. "Some of you already know us, but let me introduce our group to you new people. My name is Chris, this is Rachael, Ruth, and last of all, Ann."

They smiled at the dancers, and most of the dancers grinned back or raised their hands in a greeting.

"I'm the director of M&L Productions, the company producing the video you'll be working on," explained Chris. "It's your job to create a fantastic backing for the singer. As always in these situations, it's all about her, not you. Think of yourselves as highly talented wallpaper, if you like."

Several of the dancers laughed. Chris spoke quietly to Ann, who nodded. They both looked pleased. "Ruth will explain the concept of the video to you, after she's sorted out the costumes you'll need," said Chris. "Then Rachael will put you through your paces. Good luck, and I hope you have a great time working for us."

He and Ann left, and Ruth beckoned all the dancers into a close group in front of her.

"In this video you will have two costume changes," she told them. "First you'll be dressed as workmen, with overalls and hard hats, and in the second half you'll be wearing suits."

"I don't fancy dancing in a suit," said Luke, looking unimpressed. "Overalls sound good…but suits?"

"That's the way it has to be," said Ruth firmly. "It's to do with the song. Can't be helped I'm afraid. But they won't be proper suits. They'll be made of Lycra so you can move in them. Don't worry, we won't make life too difficult for you. Now the first thing we need to do is to get you all measured. You four, come with me. Costume fitting is next door. Okay?"

Most of the morning was taken up with sorting things out. When Marmalade went in to be measured, he found Ruth and two assistants busy with notebooks and a whole heap of costumes. "Hello," she said. "So they found us a redhead after all! I was beginning to think they'd never do it." She smiled at Marmalade and he smiled back. So *that's* why he had been picked! For a moment he felt rather foolish that he'd spent so much time worrying that his look would be wrong. In fact it was just right. How lucky was that!

"Go to Seb for measuring and then Beth will find you some overalls," Ruth told him. Beth gave Marmalade overalls and a bright yellow hard hat and told him to write his name on the labels inside. The suits would have to be hired especially to fit each dancer, so there was nothing else to try on just now.

As soon as everyone had been fitted, they met again in the practice room for Ruth to explain the video.

"Okay," she said. "We need you in two groups. The singer will be sitting on some scaffolding in the first half of the song, and you'll be dancing behind her and underneath her too. You'll be weaving in and out of the scaffolding, leaning on shovels and hauling stuff up and down."

"Sounds good," said Rich, a dancer with long, very striking, blonde hair.

"Okay. Let's have a go at blocking this first section out," suggested Rachael. "Getting your starting positions sorted out is vital. Paz, Stevie, Katie and you, sorry I don't know your name," she said to Marmalade.

Marmalade told her and she smiled at him. "Cool name! Okay. You go and join Paz's group, and… Donna, can you join them too?"

Soon, Marmalade was walking through a sequence of moves with the others. They had to imagine most of the set. They were allowed to wear the hard hats but as yet there was no scaffolding, and no props.

Marmalade was pleased about the hats. "They make it easier to get into the role, don't they?" he said to Donna.

She nodded. "Much easier," she agreed.

In the second section of the video the dancers had to walk about in front of a screen.

It was hard work getting the choreography to look exactly how the production company wanted it. Rachael and Ruth took time to stand back and consider the look of the piece. Several times they moved some people into new positions and swapped others around. Once they'd got everyone how they wanted them they put on a tape with a stonking beat, and walked them through all their steps. There were no cameras of course, because this was just a practice room, but the atmosphere was electric. Everyone was serious about making the routine the best it could be, but they were having fun too. Marmalade found himself at the front, which was a bit scary because it meant he couldn't follow anyone else. But both Rachael and Ruth seemed pleased with them all.

"I think we've done enough for today," said Ruth at last. "And we won't need to meet again until the sets are built at the film studio and the suits are ready. Once that's all happened we'll meet there to rehearse instead of in this practice room. So we'll be in touch."

Most of the dancers went downstairs to find their minders. Mrs. Player was sitting with several other teachers and parents. She looked as if she'd had fun as well.

"Okay?" she asked as Marmalade reached her.

"Great!" he said. "I've really enjoyed myself."

"Good," she said. "Let's go then."

"See you next time!" called Nina.

It didn't take long to get back to school. But during

the drive Marmalade was very quiet. He was tired after all his hard work at the rehearsal, but, as he relaxed, a thought hit him. He reached for his phone and texted Pop.

Meet me in the hall in a couple of minutes, he wrote. *Just had a great idea for the prom!*

6 A Horrible Argument

Marmalade could see Pop waiting for him outside the main school building. He thanked Mrs. Player, and scrambled out of the car. He ran over to Pop and caught her sleeve.

"How did you get on?" she asked.

"Brilliant!" he said. "It was brilliant!" Then he paused. "But when I got there everyone was like me...wild hair and very tall." He looked awkward. "And then one of the video people told me that she was pleased they'd found a red-headed dancer at last. Don't laugh!" he told Pop, crossly. "I thought I must have got in because I was the best dancer in our class, but obviously I didn't. I don't know what to say to Martin and Ellie now. It's embarrassing."

"Well don't say anything then," Pop advised him. "And you don't need to look so upset. Given that the scout was only seeing talented dancers, she was bound to choose the ones with the right look. It happens all the time in modelling. This time you got lucky. Next time it'll probably be someone else."

"I suppose," said Marmalade, brightening up. "I ought to be grateful I got lucky, instead of worrying about it."

"Absolutely!" said Pop firmly. "Now, tell me about this idea of yours."

"Did you get my text?" he asked.

"Duh!" laughed Pop. "I wouldn't be hanging around here if I hadn't, would I? There's a film on in the theatre, and we're missing it!"

"Oh, sorry," said Marmalade.

"It's okay," said Pop. "I've seen it before and it's not so brilliant that I'd want to see it again. So, what's this big idea for the prom?"

"Well," explained Marmalade. "It suddenly came to

me on the way back from the rehearsal. We're doing this really cool bit in the video where we all wear overalls and hard hats and stuff. We need to decorate the hall and the dining room for the prom, don't we?"

"Ye-es."

"Well!" Marmalade dragged Pop in through the huge double doors and into the imposing hall with the stairs sweeping up in front of them. "This is where everything starts off, isn't it?" he said. "The prom king waits at the bottom of the stairs and the prom queen comes down to meet him and they start off the dancing."

He twirled her round but Pop pushed him away. She was beginning to look a bit impatient. "I know all that," she told him. "Dancing is here and food in the dining room. So?"

"Think of it!" said Marmalade. "We'd only need some of that yellow 'men at work' tape. And I expect the ground staff could lend us a few barrows and tools to scatter around. It would be perfect! And so easy to do. Well within our budget too."

Pop stared at him. "You're proposing to scatter

tools and stuff around for us to trip over, and call it decorations?"

Marmalade nodded excitedly. "But that's not all," he insisted, thinking she was being very slow. "We were trying to come up with a good theme, weren't we? I thought of street, but this develops that idea really well. 'Men at Work'! We can all wear overalls and hard hats. I'm sure we can find some easily. They don't need to be proper ones. Don't joke shops and toyshops do all sorts of hats? And we can have funky tunes, and fast food." He paused. "I wonder if we could decorate the serving hatch so it looks like a burger van?" He bit his lip. "Maybe the art department could do that?" He beamed at Pop enthusiastically. "It'll be *so* different. Everyone will remember it for ever!"

Pop stared at him.

"Well, what's the matter?" he said. "It's different, isn't it? You wanted something different."

"Not *that* different," she snapped. "It's a stupid idea. No one will want to wear horrible old overalls. Both Lolly and I are going for prom queen, and so is Chloe.

We want to look glamorous! I'm going to put my hair up. The girls won't want to wear ridiculous hard hats. They would *ruin* their hairstyles!"

She tapped him imperiously on his chest. "Martin and Jack are both going for prom king as well as some of the other boys. Think how elegant they'll look all dressed up, especially Jack. I've seen his poster. It's over there." She pointed at the noticeboard but Marmalade ignored her. "He's stuck a photo of himself in evening dress on it," she went on. "And he looks gorgeous! No one is going to vote for you if you tell them you're coming in *overalls*!"

Pop folded her arms and glared at Marmalade. "We need a theme, not a building site. And we need something special to eat, not burgers! You've got carried away with your rehearsal this afternoon. No doubt that was all great fun and everything, but we're not making a video. We're trying to organize a prom. The girls will want to wear their best dresses and the boys will expect to wear suits and bow ties."

Marmalade was hurt. He hated having his idea shot

down by Pop. He had been so sure she'd think it was clever and different. He didn't want them to seriously fall out, but he had to let her know he was fed up with her attitude. Even so, he tried to keep his voice light and jokey for his reply. "Well you obviously can't think past the end of your nose!" he told her. "It's a great idea, but you're too dozy to see it."

Pop didn't seem to understand that Marmalade hadn't intended this as a serious insult. "Don't call me dozy!" she shouted. "How dare you."

Marmalade hadn't meant to lose his temper, but he shouted back, "Well you must be if you can't see how good my idea is."

It was all going horribly wrong. If people weren't open to new ideas nothing would ever change. Long dresses and bow ties were all very well, but every year was the same. They'd discussed so many themes, and none of them had seemed right. Now he'd come up with a cracker of an idea and she was shooting it down in flames!

Marmalade thought about some of the ideas they'd

already discarded. Pop's favourite up until now had been a golden theme, but they'd shelved that as it didn't seem exciting enough. "I know!" he told her, calming down a little. "You liked the golden idea, didn't you?"

Pop nodded cautiously.

"Well this would be a perfect way to get everyone to wear gold," he told her. "All we have to do is put some glitter on the hats!" he threw his arms out dramatically. "Just imagine!" he said. "A sea of glittering, golden heads…"

He looked at her hopefully. Surely that would win her over. But Pop looked deeply unimpressed.

"If you think the committee is going to ask people to wear hard hats with a bit of glitter on for the Lower School Prom you've got another think coming," she told him in a steely voice. She glared at him for a moment and then turned on her heel and started walking down the corridor towards the small theatre.

"Where are you going?" asked Marmalade plaintively.

Pop paused and turned to look at him again. "As I'm obviously too dozy for you I'm going to go and watch the film," she said. "Watching a mediocre movie for the second time is better than being insulted any day."

She carried on walking and Marmalade let her go. Perhaps calling her dozy had been a bit mean, but why couldn't she have taken it as a joke? She wasn't usually so touchy. Marmalade was still angry at the way she had treated his idea, too. Even if she hadn't liked it she could have let him down gently. Maybe it wasn't what she had expected for the prom, but at least it was something new!

Marmalade stood in front of Jack's poster and frowned. He did look good in his suit, but so would everyone else. He decided to go back to his room and shower. Then he'd make *his* prom king poster. Marmalade didn't have any pictures of himself dressed up, but he did have what he hoped was a big advantage. Surely everyone would want him, the pop video king, to start off the dancing? Neither Martin nor Jack could compete with that!

He wrote: *Vote for Marmalade! Pop video prom king!* on a large piece of paper. Marmalade was still in a huff with Pop, but he was sure that when his roommates turned up he'd get some sympathy. Danny would understand. He would see how horrible Pop was being, and what a great idea Marmalade had come up with. It was time they had a cool *boys'* theme. And if Pop didn't like it, that was just too bad!

7 A Surprise for Marmalade

To Marmalade's astonishment, Danny, Ed and Ben didn't side with him straight away.

"But the girls like to dress up," said Ben with a shrug.

"I don't mind what we do," said Ed, "as long as the food is good."

Marmalade looked at Danny but Danny held up his hands. "I'm not taking sides," he said firmly. "I like the easy life! You and Pop are as bad as each other. You were inseparable until tonight. Now you're worst enemies. You'll probably be best friends again tomorrow. Come on. Tell us something good, like how your rehearsal went today."

Dancing Star

Marmalade felt better after talking about the rehearsal. But he was still upset at Pop's attitude to his "Men at Work" idea. And it seemed that neither was willing to give way and make up. For the next few days, Marmalade stuck with the boys, and Pop spent all her time with her sister Lolly, Tara or Chloe.

To make matters worse, it was the week when they'd organized the voting for the prom king and queen. Loads of posters had gone up asking for support, and the school was buzzing with people trying to decide who to vote for. Marmalade knew he should have been out canvassing for support, but since falling out with Pop the whole idea of the prom had rather soured for him. He'd stuck his poster up anyway, but didn't have the heart to make much more effort. In a tiny corner of his mind he acknowledged that maybe she'd been right about the theme. Perhaps his idea hadn't been *that* good. But he still couldn't forgive her for being so horrible about it. And Pop didn't seem likely to forgive Marmalade for insulting her, especially if he didn't apologize. It was deadlock.

A Surprise for Marmalade

At the end of the week, all the votes were counted by the teachers, and the results put up on the noticeboard. Marmalade wasn't even going to go and look, but the rest of his roommates wanted to see the results, so he drifted over to the hall with them.

"It's you!" said Danny as soon as they reached the noticeboard.

Marmalade was astonished. "It can't be!" he said. He couldn't help feeling pleased, especially as he hadn't done anything to try and win support. "Who's the queen?" he asked. "Is it Chloe?"

"No," said Danny, beginning to laugh. "It's not."

"Who is it then?" he asked. "Why are you laughing? It's not someone who's a terrible dancer, is it?"

"No!" said Danny. "She's really good at dancing. Look for yourself."

He moved out of the way and Marmalade stared at the notice. "You did this on purpose to get us to make up!" he stormed. "I can't have Pop as my prom queen. She'll probably stamp on my feet with her spiky heels and ruin everything!"

Ben laughed. "Don't be ridiculous," he said. "Loads of us wanted to be prom king, but you won. Lucky you! Perhaps you got the most votes because you and Pop got the organization going when everyone else was too involved with their exams to bother. Loads of people have been saying how good it was that you started the 'ball rolling'!"

"Huh!" Marmalade was really disappointed, and didn't find Ben's joke very funny. "Some reward! Why couldn't I have had Chloe, or Lolly...even Tara would have been better than Pop!"

"Thanks!" said Tara, who was walking past and overheard the conversation.

Marmalade groaned. "Sorry!" he said. "I didn't mean..."

"I know what you meant," said Tara with a wry smile. "Don't worry. But you can't have a prom queen who doesn't like dancing very much. I can't dance to save my life, and I don't care! Look on the bright side," she added. "Perhaps knowing you *have* to dance together will get you to make up. I'm fed up of Pop constantly moaning about you. All you have to do is say sorry for calling her dozy. I'm sure she'd make up with you then."

"You called her dozy?" said Ed, his eyes wide with appalled delight. "You've done it now, mate. She'll never speak to you again."

"I don't care," said Marmalade. But he did care. He hated how they passed each other in the corridor and looked the other way. And he hated how Pop would fall silent when she noticed him nearby. That was all bad enough, but things were about to get a whole lot worse.

Marmalade was still in the hall with his friends when Pop came storming in. She went up to the noticeboard and stared at the results for a moment, before turning away, her face like thunder.

It was awful. Usually, everybody *wanted* to be voted prom king or queen. And both Marmalade and Pop usually loved to be the centre of attention, but not now. Not with each other.

Marmalade watched Pop warily as she came over to him.

"Come over here," she said, dragging him off to a quiet part of the hall so they could have a private conversation. "Well?" she said in a stony voice.

"Well what?" he said huffily.

"What are we going to do about this?" She nodded in the direction of the results, and stood there, arms folded, glaring at him.

"It's not *my* fault," said Marmalade.

Pop rolled her eyes. "I didn't say it was," she told him. "But we've got to deal with it."

Marmalade shrugged. "I'll be there in my hard hat and overalls," he told her. "It's up to you what you do."

"You can't be prom king in *overalls*!" she told him. "Besides, the committee hasn't finalized the theme yet, and there's no *way* it'll be your stupid plan, so you absolutely *won't* be allowed to wear overalls."

"I'm not dictating what *you* wear," he pointed out. "So you shouldn't dictate to *me*."

Pop was speechless for a moment and Marmalade pressed home his advantage.

"If you don't like it you don't have to turn up," he added. "Or maybe *I* won't."

"You can't not turn up!" Pop said, looking aghast. "I can't start the dancing on my own! How humiliating would that be?"

Marmalade simply shrugged. He was feeling quite pleased with himself, when he noticed a tear roll down Pop's cheek. Maybe he had gone too far? He could see that Pop was really upset, when normally she was so feisty. But while he was trying to decide what to say she spoke again.

"You're horrible," she told him. "You're spoiling everything. You only think of yourself and you don't care how anybody else feels. I hate you." Her voice broke and she ran quickly through the double doors and out into the garden.

Marmalade felt awful, but he was still annoyed. He hadn't wanted Pop to get tearful. There was no need for that. His friends had already gone, so he stuck his hands in his pockets and sauntered back to his room, trying to look as if he didn't care.

He didn't mention the latest argument to Danny, and put it to the back of his mind. By the time they went over for tea he had managed to convince himself that it hadn't been much of an argument at all.

He and Danny got in the queue for food, laughing and joking as usual, when Ellie joined them.

"I don't know what *you've* got to laugh about," she said to Marmalade.

Marmalade looked at her in astonishment. "What's up with you?" he asked.

"*You!*" she told him. "Since that scout came, Martin and I have been trying to work out how we could improve ourselves in future. We assumed you'd got picked because you were a better dancer than us in some way. We even wondered if we ought to have made an effort with our clothes, like you did. But you were only chosen because you have long red hair! Well thanks a lot. You could have told us!"

"But...I..."

"You needn't deny it," she added. "Pop told me. And the stupid thing is, if only you'd *said*, we'd have been fine about it. But to give the impression that you were the best when it simply wasn't true. How *could* you? It's so shallow."

"I didn't!" protested Marmalade. "And if you'd *asked* I'd have…" but she pushed past him and took her food, before storming back to her table.

"Well!" said Danny. "What's up with you these days, Marmalade? You can't seem to do *anything* right!"

"It's not *me*!" said Marmalade crossly. "It's everyone *else*." But inside he was kicking himself for confiding in Pop. He *should* have told his classmates, however awkward he'd felt about it, but he'd taken *her* advice not to. Now she'd really dropped him in it! Martin and Jack would be annoyed with him for not owning up as well as Ellie, and he hadn't really meant to deceive them. He just hadn't thought about how they might feel.

Marmalade was fed up with being disliked. But there was a convenient person to blame instead of himself for all his troubles. Yes. It was obviously Pop's fault!

8 A Horrible Meeting

All in all, Marmalade's life wasn't exactly going to plan. For the first time ever he wasn't looking forward to his dance class. And when he got there everyone *was* pretty annoyed with him, although it didn't last. Luckily, his classmates weren't the sort of people to bear grudges.

"I didn't think you'd be worrying about how to improve for next time," he explained. "I was too busy feeling awkward about how I'd been picked *this* time. I'm sorry."

"And I shouldn't have been so angry with you earlier," Ellie told him. "I jumped to conclusions when Pop told me. It was just a misunderstanding, wasn't it?"

A Horrible Meeting

"Yes." Marmalade was grateful they were friends again, but even more annoyed with Pop. Unfortunately, at lunchtime there was a meeting of the prom committee, and he wasn't looking forward to that one bit.

As soon as morning school was over, he made his way to the dining room for the meeting. Marmalade had had terrible trouble getting boys to join in. After the exams, Danny had eventually agreed to help, but most of the committee members were girls, and Marmalade was sure they'd all take Pop's side in every decision that had to be made. Today they had to settle on a theme, so everything else could be organized around it, and Marmalade was sure the discussion would not be good-natured.

Luckily, Danny was already there, so Marmalade made for the empty chair between him and Chloe. Unfortunately, as he approached, Pop plonked herself down in the chair. "Oh, you're not sitting there, are you?" Marmalade said, offhandedly. He loitered, hoping she'd move, but she didn't, and suddenly, most of the places around the table seemed to be taken.

Pop turned and looked daggers at him. "I'm sitting with my friends," she told him. "You can sit over the other side."

Marmalade didn't mean to snap, but his dance lesson had been awkward because of her and he couldn't keep his temper. "A fine friend *you* turned out to be," he told her. "Betraying things said in confidence."

Pop looked embarrassed. "Oh *that,*" she said. "I only let it slip out by mistake because I was so angry with you."

"Well now I'm angry with you," he told her. "You're not just dozy, but a useless friend as well. I'd be surprised if *anyone* trusted you with a secret from now on."

Pop gave a gasp and turned pale. Her sister and Chloe glared at Marmalade. Tara spoke up. "Come on," she said. "We have a meeting to run and decisions to make. Either sit down and shut up, or leave."

For a moment Marmalade hesitated. He was tempted to go, but that would be giving in. Besides, it wouldn't be fair on Danny, after Marmalade had leaned on him to take part. Slowly, Marmalade moved round the table, found a spare seat and sat down. He put his hands in his pockets and leaned back in his chair, trying to look nonchalant.

"Do you want me to start things off?" Tara asked Pop, who usually took charge of meetings.

Pop shook her head. "It's okay," she said in a small voice. She unfolded a piece of paper and cleared her throat. "We don't have much time, so we need to take a vote on the theme," she said more confidently. "These are the suggestions we've had," she said. "'Golden', 'Black and White', 'James Bond'…" She hesitated for a second. "'Men at Work'…and 'The Thirties'. Hands up for 'Golden'."

A couple of people raised their hands. Not many liked "Black and White", but a few voted for "James Bond". Then it came to "Men at Work". Marmalade was the only person to vote for his idea. He pushed his chair back and stood up. "Well, as it's all obviously rigged I'm out of here," he said. He stormed over to the serving hatch, which had just opened, and got his lunch. He took it over to the other side of the room and sat at an empty table. He knew he shouldn't have said what he had, but Pop made him so cross he was getting into the habit of saying stupid things.

After a while, Danny came over and joined him. "You have to apologize," Danny told him quietly.

"I just keep making things worse, don't I?" admitted Marmalade.

"Well why not just apologize and make up, then?" said Danny.

"Why doesn't she?" demanded Marmalade.

"I'm sure she will if you do," said Danny. "You know how much she likes you. But she doesn't have so much to apologize for, and you've really upset her. It's unkind to make people cry."

Marmalade groaned. "Everybody's *at* me all the time," he complained. "I'm not *that* horrible, am I?"

"Not when you stop being so stubborn you're not," said Danny. "You've just backed yourself into a corner, and you don't know how to get out of it. Go and make things up with Pop. Hurry up, or this prom will be the worst one ever." He looked at Marmalade. "Please?"

Marmalade sighed. "All right," he agreed. "I'll apologize if you think I should. But not in the dining room, not in front of everyone," he added fiercely. "Tell her to meet me by the lake, and not to bring any of her mates with her. This is between me and Pop, not the rest of the world!"

He abandoned his lunch and walked quickly out of the dining room. He headed for the lake and walked round to the far side, where he sat on a bench to wait. Maybe she wouldn't come. He wasn't sure whether he wanted her to or not. He wasn't looking forward to apologizing, but in his heart he knew that it was the right thing to do. It was stupid to let this feud continue. Besides, he didn't like making her cry. He just didn't know how to react when she did.

It was hot in the sun. Marmalade hoped she'd come quickly if she *was* going to come. He could already feel the sun burning his pale skin. If she didn't appear soon he'd have to find some shade. And besides, it would be the beginning of afternoon school soon. He stood up impatiently and shaded his eyes from the sun. And then he saw her. Pop was making her way towards him, and she was alone.

9 An Uneasy Truce

"Well? What do you want?" Pop's eyes were red, but she wasn't crying. In fact she looked very determined. Marmalade swallowed. The sooner he got it over with the better.

"I just wanted us to make up," he said, shrugging uncomfortably. "It's stupid to keep quarrelling, isn't it?"

"It's not nice falling out," she agreed, warily.

"I'm sorry." There. He'd said it. Thank goodness. Now they could go back to being friends. But it seemed Pop wasn't going to let him off the hook as easily as that.

"What for?" she asked.

Marmalade took a deep breath. It didn't actually

hurt, this apologizing business. But it was hard work. He had to grit his teeth to get the words out.

"For calling you dozy," he told her, "…and about the theme votes. I know they weren't rigged. Sorry."

"I'm sorry too," she told him straight away. "For telling Ellie what you told me about being chosen for the video. I shouldn't have done it, but I was so angry with you it just slipped out."

"That's all right," said Marmalade. "It doesn't matter." He smiled ruefully. "I think they've all forgiven me now."

She met his smile, and for a moment neither of them spoke. Then they both started to say something at the same time and laughed.

"You first," said Marmalade.

"I was just going to tell you about the exam results," she said. "Mrs. Pinto was putting them up on the board when I came out of the dining room."

"Really?" Marmalade was fairly certain he didn't want her to tell him what he'd got, especially for maths, but he tried to force his face into a vaguely interested expression.

"No. It's good news!" she told him. "Our revision paid off."

"It did?"

"Well, mainly with history, geography and science," she admitted. "But listen. In history I got sixty-three per cent and you got sixty-four!"

"Really?" Marmalade couldn't help grinning. "You're not kidding me?" he asked.

"No!" said Pop. "Honestly. You can go and see for yourself. Isn't it great?"

"Yeah." They exchanged grins, and Marmalade felt his troubles sliding off him. Things were looking up. But Pop hadn't quite finished.

"The prom theme," she said. "After you'd gone we finished voting and 'The Thirties' was the theme that won hands down. I hope you don't mind too much."

"It's okay," he said. "I've decided what to do."

She looked at him anxiously. He hadn't really decided. Or at least it had just occurred to him. He couldn't be bothered with it any more. He just wanted to get rid of all the hassles.

"I don't mind the theme being 'The Thirties'," he told her.

"Really?" Pop's face lit up. She looked so happy. "That's brilliant, Marmalade. Thanks. I'll tell you what we thought then. Lolly and I are singing this thirties song for the end of term concert. We were doing a bit of research for the song and discovered all these wonderful clothes and music. The men wore such cool suits, and the women had amazing dresses. It was just before the Second World War. We can have long cigarette holders, without cigarettes of course," she giggled. "And fruit cocktails, and we can talk in posh accents. You'll have to watch an old film on the internet. They're brilliant!"

"Yes, well. I expect they are," said Marmalade, feeling pretty miffed that she'd already worked out so much for the theme. "But I won't watch a film thanks, because I won't need to know anything about the period."

Something in his voice gave her reason to pause. She looked at him with a mixture of surprise and concern.

"You won't?"

"Nah. You can find someone else to be on the committee. I've gone off the idea."

Pop looked shocked. But she recovered herself. "Well, okay," she told him. "I'm sorry. It would have been great doing it with you. But I can understand if you'd rather not."

"Yeah," he said. "I'd rather not."

There was a brief silence.

"But you'll still come?" she said. "You'll still be the prom king?"

"Of course!" he said. "Simple, isn't it? If you want to have a thirties theme, that's fine by me. I'll come as a thirties workman."

Pop's face fell. "Marmalade, please," she begged. "You can't do that."

"Why not?" he asked. "They must have had workmen in the thirties. I tell you what. I'll get a flat cap instead of a yellow hat. I don't suppose they had plastic hats in those days, did they?"

"But I'll be wearing a long dress!" she said.

Marmalade shrugged. "You can't have *everything* your own way," he told her. "You get to have a theme you like, but if I want to wear overalls I'll wear them, and there's nothing you can do about it. Sorry."

He felt bad about leaving her looking so forlorn, but it seemed fair enough. She could have her theme, and organize it the way she wanted to. He'd apologized to her for being rude. What more did she want?

He breezed his way back towards the schoolhouse, and found Danny sitting on a wall with Tara.

"Well?" said Danny.

Marmalade pushed his hair out of his eyes. "All done," he told Danny, trying to remain nonchalant. "It's almost time for lessons. Shall we go in?"

For the rest of the afternoon it was impossible for Danny to ask Marmalade what had happened at the lake. Marmalade paid attention in lessons, and smiled at Pop when she happened to look his way. He ignored the fact that she looked almost as unhappy as she had done before he'd apologized. He kept telling himself how reasonable he had been, and almost managed to convince himself. But Danny had a different opinion once they could talk.

"You're just being mean," Danny told Marmalade when he'd found out the truth.

"How is it mean to give in on everything except what I wear?" asked Marmalade. "I don't want to hire a dinner jacket and stuff."

"Everyone else will," Ed pointed out.

"That doesn't mean I have to," insisted Marmalade. He wouldn't be swayed.

Marmalade spent the next couple of days trying to pretend he wasn't being stubborn over his prom clothes. But the more his friends tried to persuade him to change his mind, the more stubborn he became. One afternoon he met Ellie on the path.

"How's it going?" she asked him.

"Fine," he said. "I should be getting a call for the video rehearsals soon. I can't wait to have a run-through on the set, once it's built."

"I'm glad you're so happy, Marmalade," she said. "As you are, do you think you could make someone else happy too?"

"Of course!" said Marmalade. "Anything I can do! What's the problem?"

"It's not me," she told him. "It's Pop. She's really stressing about the first prom dance. The one she has to do with you."

"Oh." Marmalade's heart sank. It had been bad enough to have Chloe, Lolly and Tara getting at him, but now Ellie was joining in, and she wasn't even particularly friendly with Pop.

"It wouldn't hurt you to hire a dinner jacket, would it?" she went on. "All the other boys are…and you're going to be prom king."

"But I've given way on everything else!" he protested.

"So you're saying you won't?" she said.

Marmalade nodded. "Absolutely!" he told her. "I'm standing up for my rights."

"No you're not," she told him coldly. "You're being an idiot."

An Uneasy Truce

She turned on her heel and strode away. Marmalade watched her go anxiously. Was he wrong to stand firm on this? He wasn't sure. But surely he shouldn't allow himself to be pushed around? He'd made up his mind and, even if it wasn't the best decision in the world, he was within his rights to make it. No. Even if the whole school turned against him, Marmalade Stamp would never change his mind.

10 Rehearsal Time

A couple of days later, Marmalade got the call to go for a video rehearsal. As he headed out to the car with his water bottle and towel, he saw Mr. Penardos.

"Good luck this afternoon," said his teacher.

"Thanks," said Marmalade. "We'll be in the studio this time, so I'm really excited."

"Meanwhile I have had an invitation to the Lower School Prom, which is also exciting," Mr. Penardos told Marmalade, with a smile. "I look forwar' to it very much. And I understand you will be prom king. Congratulations!"

"Thanks," said Marmalade again.

"I look forwar' to seeing you lead the first dance,"

continued Mr. Penardos. "Pop is a good dancer, and I think you will both look so elegant, no?"

"Er…yes," said Marmalade, awkwardly.

He got into the car thinking hard. He couldn't pretend that dancing with Pop while wearing overalls would make either of them look elegant. But he still wasn't ready to give in. How could he make her smile instead of cry when she saw him at the bottom of the stairs, waiting for her? On his way to the rehearsal he tried to think of how he could have his own way and bring a smile to Pop's face. He usually found it easy to make people laugh, but not this time. Well, he would just have to hope he'd come up with something that would please them both.

It was good to be with the video dancers again, and fantastic to be able to rehearse on the set. Marmalade hadn't been inside a proper film studio before. Both of the sets had been built inside a huge room. On one side was the scaffolding, built on a floor painted to look like a grey, dusty building site. But the backdrop was brilliant white. Marmalade supposed that white was so they would stand out well in their dark overalls and yellow hats. A little way off was the other set. It was much simpler, just a painted backdrop of a modern city skyline, and the floor was made to look like a pavement. It was really cool.

"Have you any idea what the song is about?" Marmalade asked Nina. "We've only heard the tune so far."

"Not a clue," she told him, with a grin. "But who cares? It's fun, isn't it?"

They went through their paces for Rachael. The stonking beat for the scaffolding part came blasting out of a couple of huge speakers. The music was vital, so they could get their timing just right. It wasn't so easy now they had to cope with the set as well. If one of them missed catching the right piece of scaffolding, everyone would be thrown out of sync.

Ruth got them all to try their boots, which made an enormous difference to the way they danced. Marmalade found himself stamping through the routine with gusto. And he found he would mostly be performing under the scaffolding, directly below the singer.

"Ace position," said Gav, one of the other dancers. "I bet we'll be in shot for most of this section. That won't do our profiles any harm at all."

"Let's go through that one more time," yelled Rachael over the enthusiastic stamping of feet. "Gav, Bex, Neil and Marmalade, I'd like you to jump up onto that bit of scaffolding for a count of five after the hammer sounds come in." She counted them through it and Marmalade took off at precisely the right time.

"Good!" she yelled. "Well done, Marmalade. Too slow, the rest of you."

They went over it several times until everyone had it spot on.

After a break they tried on the suits. "Excellent!" said Ruth, satisfied by how smart they looked.

They weren't allowed to wear the suits for the practice, in case they got damaged before the shoot, but it didn't matter. There was so little to do, and it wasn't difficult. The second half of the tune was cool, laid-back music and they simply had to wander about in front of the backdrop, holding laptop cases, or mobile phones. Of course, it was more precise than that. Rachael had marked the starting positions they'd worked out on the floor beforehand, and they had to rehearse each and every move repeatedly.

"I've never spent so much time practising such ordinary moves," said Marmalade with a laugh when they had a quick break.

"Ah!" said Paz. "That's what makes it *look* so casual and aimless. If we didn't rehearse we'd probably bump into each other and then it wouldn't look half as slick."

At the end of the rehearsal Chris came down from the control room.

"It's looking good," he told them. "I'm very pleased. Well done. We'll go for the shoot tomorrow."

The dancers exchanged excited looks. "Fantastic!" said Marmalade. "I can't wait."

On the way back to school, Marmalade decided to ask Mr. Fallon, the groundsman, if he had a pair of overalls he could lend him for the prom. Niggling away at him was the knowledge that he was making life difficult, not just for Pop, but for himself too. It would be so much easier to just give in and wear a suit like everyone else. But he pushed that thought away. Why should he do it, just because Pop wanted him to? Besides, he'd had an exciting day, and had another to look forward to tomorrow. He didn't want to be worrying about the prom when there was the filming to think about.

But now it seemed no one in the lower school had time for anything *except* the prom. Marmalade felt very left out. It had been his idea to leave the committee, but now he wished he'd stayed on board. Everyone seemed busy with the arrangements except him.

The thirties theme looked as if it was going to be a triumph. There were still a couple of days to go, but a few of the decorations were already going up in the hall and the dining room, with the help of the staff. A huge glitter ball had been hung high above the dance floor and, to make the thirties' feel just right, someone had printed out snippets they'd found on the internet. There was the first edition of *The Beano*, a picture of a beautiful ballerina, called Margot Fonteyn, and some smartly dressed theatre goers, as well as pictures of film stars and singers of the time.

"What do you think of this little noticeboard?" Ed asked Marmalade. "I thought it was important to remember that the thirties wasn't *all* glitz and glamour."

Marmalade looked at the bits and pieces Ed had put up. There was a picture of the Jarrow Crusade, when two hundred unemployed people marched from Tyneside to London. There was also a picture of Prime Minister Neville Chamberlain declaring "Peace for our time" – just before the start of the Second World War.

"I think that's good," said Marmalade, who was in a sombre mood anyway, and grateful that Ed wanted his opinion. "But I expect most people will be more interested in the film stars and musicians, than war, or unemployment."

"That's fair enough," said Ed. "It's a prom. It's *supposed* to be a fun event," he added, giving Marmalade a hard look.

When Marmalade got back to his boarding house and went up to his room, he noticed three dark suits hanging up. That gave him a shock. Somehow, although he'd known the prom was on Saturday, it hadn't quite hit home. He wouldn't have time to see Mr. Fallon about the overalls tomorrow. He'd have to go right away. Luckily, the groundsman was in his shed, just about to pack up for the day. He was kind enough to lend Marmalade a completely new pair of overalls and a hard hat. Marmalade had no idea whether they'd have looked any different in the 1930s, but he told himself the styles probably hadn't changed all that much.

"Don't you lose them mind!" Mr. Fallon warned Marmalade. "I know what you kids are like. I want them back here straight after the weekend."

On the way back to his room, Marmalade was accosted by Pop's friends.

"We saw you going over to the groundsman's shed," said Tara, looking disapprovingly at the overalls hanging over his arm.

"We want to ask you one more time to change your mind about what you're going to wear," said Chloe. "You're not being fair. You know you're not."

"Please will you reconsider?" said Lolly. "Surely there's still time to hire a suit?"

Marmalade almost wavered. Pop's sister was such a sweet person, and so was Chloe. It seemed mean to refuse their request. But Marmalade had made it absolutely clear to everyone how he felt. How could he possibly climb down now?

"Right then," snapped Tara, who wasn't known for her patience. "I've had enough of this stupidity…and you, Marmalade Stamp. Just don't come running to me when you're in trouble in the future. You can go whistle as far as I'm concerned."

She turned away, and so did the others. Chloe shot him a regretful look, but that was it.

Back in his room, Marmalade hung his prom clothes

up next to Danny's, Ed's and Ben's. The overalls looked so out of place that Marmalade couldn't help but feel a ripple of worry run up his back. In spite of his excitement about being in the video, he felt as if there was a dark cloud hanging over him, and he just couldn't shift it.

11 Video Shoot

In the morning Marmalade felt better. It was the day of the video shoot. He would miss a whole day's lessons, and that *had* to be good news. No doubt it would be hard work, but he was really looking forward to the experience of being a professional dancer.

It was also the day before the prom, and every member of the lower school was in a fever of excitement, but Marmalade wasn't involved with the final preparations at all. He swallowed his breakfast quickly and made his way to the car.

At the studio, Ruth sent everyone off to get changed and made-up. "Tom's team will soon get you ready for the cameras," she told them.

Video Shoot

In a large, well-lit room, four make-up artists waited. Marmalade's face was made up by Dan.

"Hold still," he told Marmalade. "I need to accentuate your eyes. Rosie? Got any more dark grey? The black is too strong for this dancer's colouring."

Sam, the artist furthest away, tossed a make-up stick towards Dan and he deftly caught it.

As soon as they were all ready, Rachael ran them through the scaffolding section with its thumping beat. This time Ruth sat up where the singer would be, so the dancers had someone to focus on. They were supposed to look towards her at all times.

"I don't care what you have to imagine," said Rachael, as she put them through their paces. "Just set your faces as if you're looking at something amazing and wonderful."

"You *are* amazing and wonderful, Ruth," teased Marmalade, and everyone, including Ruth, laughed.

After that part of the rehearsal was over, they had a break. Debs and Eddie, two of the studio employees, had ordered in snacks and drinks for the dancers, which were very welcome.

"It's all going really well, isn't it?" Marmalade said to Kerry, between bites of energy bar.

"I'm not sure," said Kerry. "Ruth has been stressing about the costumes. Apparently the singer wanted some last-minute changes."

"I heard that she wants red shirts with the suits, not white," Nina said. "And Ruth's really worried about it. She managed to source some, but she thinks they'll look terrible with some of us because of our colouring. But what the singer wants the singer gets. However ridiculous."

Everyone nodded seriously. And Marmalade felt rather alarmed. Red was absolutely his most hated colour. He hoped Ruth wasn't thinking of him when she mentioned that it didn't suit everybody, but red would certainly look dreadful next to his ginger hair. Suddenly the day stopped being fun and started to get worrying.

As soon as it was time to rehearse the suits section,

Marmalade was taken to one side to try on a red shirt. Ruth winced when she looked at him in it.

"Can't we just tell this singer, whoever she is, that red won't work as well as white?" said Marmalade anxiously.

"She says this is what she wants, and so we have to make it work somehow," said Ruth, sounding very harassed.

Just then, Rachael came up to them. "Chris wants to try some filters," she told Ruth, fiddling with the earpiece that connected her to Chris in the control room. "Better get everyone else into shirts and jackets too, so we can see what we can do. That looks awful," she added bluntly, looking at Marmalade. His heart stopped for a moment. He just knew that *he* was going to be the main problem, with his ginger hair and freckles.

There was lots of discussion between Rachael, Ruth and the control room, but nothing seemed to be decided. They moved Marmalade around and tried him in different positions with the lighting, but nothing seemed to work.

"Poor you!" said Nina, sympathetically, as Marmalade stood next to her for a moment in front of the painted backdrop. "All this, because some singer had a bright idea that wasn't as clever as she thought."

"I hope it doesn't end up with you having to miss the shoot," said Luke. "That would be a pity, and a pain because we'd have to do even more rehearsing to make sure we filled your space. It's going to be a long enough day as it is."

"Maybe she doesn't realize what problems we're having," suggested Marmalade, stressing about being left out. Surely he wouldn't have to miss out on the filming? He couldn't bear it if he wasn't in the video. It wouldn't be fair!

"She does know about the problems," said Nina. "She must do. I caught a glimpse of her going into the control room with Chris a while ago!"

Marmalade looked up at the control-room window. Sure enough, there *was* another person there: a girl wearing huge dark glasses. He hadn't a clue who she was, but he resented her already. "Why doesn't she just let them swap back to white then?" he said. "It's obviously the best solution."

"People like her don't worry about what's *best*," snorted Nina. "They only care about what *they* want, however stupid."

Marmalade nodded. And then he found himself staring at Nina. Hadn't people at school been saying that about *him*? He gulped. Suddenly, in a flash he could see it all. *He* was as bad as the girl in the control room. It wouldn't hurt him if he wore a dinner suit for the prom, but it would upset Pop if he didn't. And it couldn't *really* matter to the singer if the shirts were red or white, but her refusal to change her mind was causing everyone loads of hassle.

"What's the matter?" said Nina. "Are you feeling okay?"

"I'm fine," said Marmalade faintly, wondering if he might be going to be sick. "But I need to make a phone call."

Marmalade had to wait for a break in the rehearsal, but it seemed to be going on for ever. He wanted to phone the suit-hire company. The prom was tomorrow night, but surely it wasn't too late to hire a dinner jacket and bow tie? If only he could get to use his phone before the shop closed!

The decision-making about the shirts went on for *ages*. At one point he even spoke up and volunteered to count himself out of the shoot, so he could escape to the phone, but the suggestion made Rachael angry.

"Don't be ridiculous," she told him. "I'm not going to start blocking out new positions at this stage. You stay where you are."

Nina squeezed his arm. "That was noble of you," she told him, which made poor Marmalade feel worse than ever.

Texting Danny for help wasn't an option, because the studio had a strict rule about mobiles being switched off at all times on the studio floor.

At long last, word came through from the control room that the decision had been reversed. Nobody cheered. Nobody wanted to risk annoying the singer so that she changed her mind again! But a huge sigh went up from everyone on the studio floor, including Ruth and Rachael.

"Right," snapped Rachael. "Dancers, fifteen-minute break. Crew, let's get tidied up and ready to roll."

Marmalade didn't hesitate. He charged down the stairs and into the lobby to use his phone.

12 Panic!

Marmalade didn't have a clue about the hire shop's phone number. He was beginning to panic when he noticed a scruffy phone book on a shelf by the door. It was out of the school's area, but if he could get a suit delivered here, to the studio, all would be well. He'd worry about returning it afterwards. He found the section on clothes hire, and tapped out the number on his mobile.

While he waited to be connected his heart was thumping and he felt so agitated he couldn't stand still. *Please pick up the phone,* he thought. *Please!*

It felt like hours, but after a few seconds the call was answered. *Thank goodness!* thought Marmalade, but his relief was short-lived.

"I'm sorry," said the lady in the hire shop. "We need at least forty-eight hours' notice for most suit hire and we don't have anything in stock that would fit you."

"What about other places?" Marmalade asked desperately. "Would other hire companies need so much time?"

"I really couldn't say," the lady answered. "But I think it's most unlikely you'll find anything at this late stage. If you'd come to us a week ago we might have been able to help."

There weren't that many hire companies in the book but Marmalade went through every one. None of them could help.

He put the phone book back on the shelf and shoved his mobile back in his pocket. There must be something he could do. There *must* be. But he couldn't think of anything. He mentally ran through all the clothes he had at school. There was nothing even vaguely suitable. He had a pair of black shoes, but that was all. He couldn't possibly turn up to the prom wearing jeans, a tracksuit or shorts. He'd almost be better off wearing the overalls! But no. He realized now how pig-headed he'd been. He wanted to put things right between him and Pop, and wearing the right clothes was the way to do it. There had to be a way round the problem, if only he could think of it.

He rushed back to the studio.

"Hurry up, Marmalade," hissed Kerry. "We're doing another walk-through in costume. Go and get changed."

Ruth handed him his clothes and Marmalade scrambled into them.

"Okay. Positions," yelled Rachael. "Let's get this show on the road."

It was a relief to have a white shirt on again. The walk-through went well, and both Ruth and Rachael were very pleased. All the comments coming down into Ruth's earpiece seemed to be positive too.

"Okay. We're going for a take on this one," said Ruth. "We'll do the scaffolding shoot afterwards. Can we have make-up on set, please?"

Tom and his make-up team appeared and touched up everyone's faces. As soon as they'd finished, Ruth told the dancers to take their positions in front of the painted backdrop.

"Stand by," said Ruth. "Take one. Cameras rolling?" She looked at each of the cameramen in turn and then spoke again. "Cameras rolling. Action."

The music started, and Marmalade moved forward with the rest of the dancers. Fortunately, they were all supposed to be looking serious and purposeful in this section. Marmalade knew he could never have put on a happy face. He was too worried about not having a suit for the prom. Then it hit him. Why not borrow the suit he was wearing? It wasn't a proper, tailored suit. It had been made in a stretchy fabric with dancers in mind. But it would be better than nothing!

He tried hard to concentrate, but he couldn't avoid a slow smile from creeping across his face.

"Cut!" Rachael wasn't looking too pleased. "*Serious* expressions, please," she told them, looking hard at Marmalade. "Back to starting positions, please. Take two."

Marmalade took a deep breath. His problem was sorted. Now he needed to put all his concentration into this take. It wasn't very professional to let his mind wander. So as soon as the cameras started rolling he became totally focused. The moves came easily to him now, and he was so involved in the performance that he was surprised when a voice suddenly shouted, "Cut!"

Paul and Dave, on the cameras, stopped filming. Rachael was waiting to hear what they thought in the control room. After a few minutes she smiled delightedly. "Amazing! Well done, guys," she said. "That's a wrap."

Luke thumped Marmalade on his back. "Well done us," he said, with a broad grin on his face.

"Yes," said Marmalade with relief that he hadn't let them down again.

The atmosphere had really lifted in the studio, with everyone feeling very positive.

"I know it's getting late," said Ruth. "And I expect

you're all getting hungry again. There's pizza coming, but let's see if we can avoid things dragging on. Shall we say a fifteen-minute break, while we get the camera positions right for the next section?"

Everyone nodded. The dancers changed into their overalls, ready for the scaffolding take, and grabbed drinks while they waited for the pizza. Marmalade took the opportunity to go and speak to Ruth about his suit. She listened carefully to his request and then shook her head.

"Sorry," she said. "Can't do it. All the costumes have been hired from a theatrical company in the city. We pay by the day, and there are big penalties if they aren't returned in time. They have to be back first thing in the morning. And even if the timescale was right, we still wouldn't let any costumes out of the studio. Too many things can go wrong. It's just not our policy."

"But this is an emergency!" he told her. "Can't you make an exception? I'd really look after it."

"No," said Ruth. "I'm sorry. Why didn't you hire a proper suit in time?"

Marmalade blushed. He didn't want to admit to Ruth how stupid he'd been. "There was a bit of a mix-up," he mumbled.

"Well that's a shame," she said sympathetically. "But I'm afraid sometimes you just have to live with the consequences of your actions. It's all part of growing up." She patted him kindly on the arm and moved away.

Marmalade was desperate. He'd thought it was all going to be sorted so easily, but now he was back where he'd started, with no suit and even less time to find one. He slumped to the floor and leaned his back against a chair.

Nina came over with a couple of slices of pizza and handed him one. "You're rather on your own over here," she commented. "Do you mind me joining you?"

"No," said Marmalade dejectedly. "It's fine."

"You don't *sound* fine though," she continued, taking a sip of her water. "Anything I can help you with?"

"Well…" Marmalade didn't really want to confide in anybody. But maybe Nina would have an idea of how he could find some suitable clothes for tomorrow night? He owed it to Pop to try anything.

"I've made a bit of a mess of things at school recently," he admitted. "And I want to put it right, but I've left it far too late."

He explained about the prom and Nina was very understanding. "I can be stubborn too," she told him. "And it's awful when you box yourself into a corner and can't get out."

Nina tried to suggest possible solutions, but by the end of the break they were no further forward.

"Well thanks for listening," Marmalade said, as they got ready to go back into the studio.

"Maybe this is one of those occasions when you just have to grovel and hope for the best," she said. "I'm sure Pop won't hate you for ever. After all, it's nearly the end of term now. By next term she'll probably have forgotten all about it."

"I doubt it," said Marmalade, gloomily.

"Well there is one thing you can do, even if you can't wear the right clothes," said Nina.

"What?"

"Get her some flowers," said Nina. "Maybe something to wear on her dress. A corsage. You know, something exotic, like an orchid. Only you'll need to find out what colour she'll be wearing, so it doesn't clash."

Marmalade managed a grateful smile. "That's a really good idea," he said. "At least it would show that I'm trying."

It was time for the scaffolding section of the song. They did a quick run-through and then the singer appeared. She'd taken off her dark glasses and was wearing a black, spangled dress. Marmalade recognized her at once. She'd had a number one a few months back. This video must be for her follow-up single! In spite of his worries Marmalade couldn't help being impressed with the job he'd landed. This video would be seen everywhere. On TV, in music shops, on the internet. It would be *huge*. And he was going to be in it!

They took their places and waited for the singer to get into position. The run-through went quite well, and Marmalade had to admit that the singer was very professional. She acted her part brilliantly. She sparkled at the cameras at just the right times, and when Marmalade and the others jumped up to swing from the scaffolding, she stared right into his eyes. He felt a jolt as their eyes met, as if she knew him, but as soon as the run-through was over, she switched off and ignored them all completely.

There was a pause, while the singer discussed how it had gone with Ruth, Rachael and Chris in the control room. Then Rachael called for the dancers' attention.

"Okay," she said. "A slight change. It's the part where you jump up onto the scaffolding and look at her. She wants you all to leap for the scaffolding but just Marmalade to hang on. You others drop off but keep your eyes on our singer. Okay?"

"What do I have to do?" asked Marmalade, anxiously.

"Just do what you did before," Rachael told him. "She liked the way you looked so yearningly at her."

"Did she?"

"Just keep yearning," said Rachael with a wry smile.

Dancing Star

"You'll be in shot, so don't mess it up."

They ran through the section again, with the cameras rolling, and Marmalade the only person staying close to the singer. The music pounded, and it felt as if the singer sang the words just for him. *"I can see that you don't belong. Follow me, it won't take long. I can make you a big tycoon, big tycoon, big tycoon."* Marmalade did his best. He'd thought his expression must be rather doleful, with his troubles weighing him down, but it was up to her if she liked it. She wasn't totally happy with her position, though, so after she'd had a brief break to adjust her make-up they went for another take.

This time, one dancer fluffed his leap and the next time another tripped over his own feet. The long day's work was having an effect on people's concentration. Rachael sent them all out of the studio to clear their heads. There was a small car park behind the studio and they wandered about there for a few minutes. It was good to have a breath of fresh air.

Marmalade noticed a bright yellow sports car.

Maybe it belonged to the singer? He thought how much Martin would have enjoyed being there. He would have appreciated the car, as well as loving being in the video.

Marmalade wished he could share his good fortune with his friends. Friends were so important. He hadn't thought about it before because he'd always had friends around. It was only since he'd fallen out with Pop, and everyone had taken her side, that he'd realized how precious friendships were. Well he'd learned an important lesson. He wouldn't take his popularity for granted any more. To have good friends you needed to *be* a good friend too. So no boasting about his role in this video, and he'd make it up to Pop somehow.

After the break things went much better. Marmalade was getting used to gazing into the singer's famous face by now, and worked hard at his yearning look. Just two more takes and Chris was happy.

"It's a wrap!" announced Ruth, with a smile. "Thank you all very much."

Dancing Star

Marmalade didn't notice the singer leave. While he was getting changed she disappeared without even saying goodbye.

Chris and Ann appeared though, and they were very enthusiastic about Marmalade's performance.

"We haven't used you before, have we?" said Ann to Marmalade.

"No," said Marmalade.

"Well we'd like to add you to our database if that's okay with you and your parents?" she asked. "We do like using Rockley Park students when we can, although we haven't needed anyone recently. Do you have an agent?"

Marmalade shook his head.

"That doesn't matter," she told him. "If we have your details on the database we can contact the school in the future if we need you. And I'm sure there will be more work for you at M&L Productions if you want it."

"Thanks!" said Marmalade, feeling very pleased.

Everyone was saying goodbye. Marmalade had mixed feelings. He was thrilled at the offer of more work in the future, but it was sad to leave the people he'd been working with, especially Nina, who'd tried to help him out.

"Bye," she said. "I'll be keeping my fingers crossed. Dance in those overalls as if they were a dinner suit and maybe what you're wearing won't matter after all."

"Thanks," said Marmalade. "For everything."

Mrs. Player was waiting for him by the studio door.

"Long day," she said. "Are you tired?"

Marmalade nodded. "It was great," he told her. "But now all I want is to get back to school."

13 A Waiting Game

Rockley Park was transformed. It was the Lower School Prom and no effort had been spared to make this a night to remember. The huge glitter ball that had been hung up a few days earlier twirled gently above everyone in the magnificent main house hall, where the dancing would take place.

The guests were welcomed with sophisticated fruit cocktails, and the kitchen staff had produced wonderful nibbles to go with them. Later, they would be serving a delicious meal as well. A Senior School swing band was entertaining early arrivals with a selection of popular thirties tunes.

The Lower School Prom started the same way every

year, and the traditional beginning was eagerly awaited by all the guests. Once everyone had arrived, the prom queen would sweep down the wide stairs to meet the prom king and they would open the proceedings by having the first dance. All eyes would be on them as they swished their way over the empty floor. It was always a big moment. Most of the students dreamed of opening the prom one day.

This year there was an even more feverish atmosphere. Almost everyone had heard of the disagreement between the king and queen. At Rockley Park nothing stayed secret for long, and everyone had an opinion about it. Some thought Marmalade should have resigned, and let another boy take his place as prom king. Most agreed that he had been voted for, so he had every right to keep his position. A few thought he was right to stand firm, but the majority were sorry that he hadn't agreed to dress up like everyone else.

But whatever thoughts they had, absolutely everyone wanted to be there to see what would happen when Marmalade came together with Pop for the first dance. So the hall was crowded, with most eyes on the staircase, while some people kept a watch for the prom king's entrance. He should be there at the bottom of the stairs, waiting for the prom queen, but so far he hadn't turned up. And the prom queen's friends were having trouble with Pop.

In the room upstairs that was always set aside as the queen's dressing room, there was a pretty arrangement of flowers on the table. In the envelope lying next to the arrangement was a little card. All it said was, "A peace offering".

"But what does it mean?" asked Pop, plaintively. "The flowers are lovely. It was sweet of him to think of them, but an arrangement in a bright yellow hard hat? What is he trying to tell me?"

"Well, he's obviously not going to wear the hat, so that's one good thing," ventured Lolly helpfully.

"It might mean he's going to stay away," suggested Tara.

Pop stared at her in horror. "Being stood up would

be even worse than having to dance with him looking ridiculous," she wailed. "I think."

"Well he's not here yet," said Chloe, who had gone to the top of the stairs to look.

"He's a good five minutes late," said Tara, looking at her watch.

Pop sank down on a chair. This was supposed to be the highlight of her term, but it was turning into a nightmare.

"What shall I do?" she asked. "How can I bear to go down those stairs with no one there to meet me? I'll feel so stupid. And I'll feel just as stupid if he turns up in those awful overalls."

Chloe went to have another look and came back looking pale. "The hall is absolutely crowded," she said. "And he's here."

14 The First Dance

Marmalade had been in a panic all day. He'd had to phone a couple of florists before he'd found one that could deliver on time. When the flowers arrived he was really pleased. He hoped they would strike just the right note. He sneaked them upstairs during the afternoon, and put them into the hard hat that he'd borrowed from Mr. Fallon. He left the card beside them. The flowers looked lovely, sitting on the table in the room Pop would use to get ready in.

Then Marmalade had disappeared for quite a while. He'd arrived back in his room while Ed, Ben and Danny were jamming over in the Rock Department, as they usually did on Saturday afternoons. By the time they arrived to shower and get changed, he was lying on his bed, trying to keep calm.

"Are you getting changed?" asked Danny, seeing that Marmalade was still in his jeans.

"Yeah. I'll go and have a shower in a minute," he said.

"What are you going to wear?" called Ed, as he went out of the door, but Marmalade pretended not to hear.

The boys would have been happy to wait for Marmalade, but he was being very slow. "You go on," he told Danny. "You're on the committee. You need to get there early."

"Are you sure?" asked Danny anxiously. "Are you all right?"

Marmalade nodded. "Just rather nervous," he laughed shakily. "I know it's not like me, but I am."

"Honestly, I don't mind waiting," said Ben. "I'll stay with you. The others can go on."

"No," said Marmalade. "You're great mates, but I think I'll be better on my own. Don't worry. I'll be there."

As soon as they'd gone Marmalade gave a big sigh. This was it. He had to get ready now. He couldn't put

Dancing Star

it off any longer. He slicked back his hair, so that it didn't fall wildly over his face any more. He looked in the mirror and a very pale, anxious face stared back at him. He was going to do his best with what he had, and hope that his best would do.

As soon as he had changed, he made his way towards the main house. The sun was getting low in the sky, and a pale light shimmered on the creamy, stone building. It was a gorgeous, warm, summer's evening. The doors were wide open, and Marmalade could hear the music. The band was playing a famous, wartime song now. He looked at his watch and broke into a run. He needed to hurry!

As he appeared at the door the students opened a path for him to the stairs. He walked through the throng with his head held high. He could hear the gasps, titters and whispers, but he ignored them. When he got to the bottom of the stairs he waited. And all the students in the hall waited with him. The music had stopped. You could have heard a pin drop.

Then Pop appeared at the top of the stairs.

The First Dance

Marmalade looked up at her and caught his breath. Pop and Lolly were models. Marmalade knew them so well he'd almost forgotten that. But tonight, dressed so beautifully in a long, slim, sea-green satin dress, Pop looked every inch the professional model. Her hair was looped up with tiny pearls, and she wore a matching necklace around her elegant neck. She looked simply perfect. For a few long seconds she paused at the top of the stairs, looking down at him. Was she going to turn on her heel and run? He thought it was entirely possible. But then she started to make her way slowly down the stairs. His heart thumped in his chest. He stood perfectly still, trying not to betray any emotion.

When she was on the last step they were exactly the same height. He stood to attention, his cap under his arm, and held out a florist's box. She took it, with a slight smile on her lips.

"Thank you," she said. "And for the flowers upstairs."

He bowed slightly, formally, from the waist.

In the box was a creamy white orchid, which matched the pearls perfectly. He took her hand, kissed it and fastened the orchid, on its band, around her wrist. She held it up to her face and looked at its luminous beauty. Then she looked straight into his eyes. There was a definite smile in hers, and his eyes were twinkling too.

"Trust you to upstage all the boys," she whispered. "Where on earth did you find it?"

Marmalade clicked his heels. "School costume department," he muttered. "The best I could do."

He was wearing the formal mess uniform of a Second World War RAF pilot. The blue-grey fitted jacket and trousers suited him tremendously.

Pop bit her lip.

"You look as if you're going to war," she told him.

Marmalade looked very serious. "I'm not *going* to war," he told her. "I'm trying to *stop* one!"

Pop laughed, and then she threw her arms round him and gave him a big hug. A couple of people let out a ragged cheer. Then someone started to clap.

In a few moments the hall was filled with the sound of applause.

Marmalade gave Pop a kiss on her cheek and she blushed. "Come on then," she told him. "Stuff arguments. Let's dance!"

✳ So you want
to be a pop star?
✳

Turn the page to read some top tips
on how to make your dreams
✳ come true... ✳

✳ Making it in the music biz ✳

Think you've got tons of talent?
Well, music maestro Judge Jim Henson,
Head of Rock at top talent academy Rockley
Park, has put together his hot tips to help
you become a superstar…

✳ Number One Rule: Be positive!
You've got to believe in yourself.

✳ Be active! Join your school choir
or form your own band.

✳ Be different! Don't be afraid to stand
out from the crowd.

✳ Be determined! Work hard and stay focused.

✳ Be creative! Try writing your own material –
it will say something unique about you.

✳ Be patient! Don't give up if things
don't happen overnight.

✳ Be ready to seize opportunities
when they come along.

✳ Be versatile! Don't have a one-track mind – try out new things and gain as many skills as you can.

✳ Be passionate! Don't be afraid to show some emotion in your performance.

✳ Be sure to watch, listen and learn all the time.

✳ Be willing to help others. You'll learn more that way.

✳ Be smart! Don't neglect your schoolwork.

✳ Be cool and don't get big-headed! Everyone needs friends, so don't leave them behind.

✳ Always stay true to yourself.

✳ And finally, and most importantly, enjoy what you do!

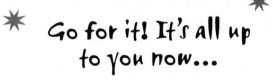

Go for it! It's all up to you now...

Usborne Quicklinks

For links to exciting websites where you can find out more about becoming a pop star and even practise your singing with online karaoke, go to the Usborne Quicklinks Website at www.usborne-quicklinks.com and enter the keywords fame school.

Internet safety

When using the Internet make sure you follow these safety guidelines:

※ Ask an adult's permission before using the Internet.

※ Never give out personal information, such as your name, address or telephone number.

※ If a website asks you to type in your name or e-mail address, check with an adult first.

※ If you receive an e-mail from someone you don't know, do not reply to it.

For more

read these other
fabulous books...

Reach for the Stars

Chloe loves singing and spends hours practising in her bedroom. So when she gets the chance to audition for Rockley Park – the school for wannabe pop stars – Chloe's determined to make the grade. But first she has to persuade her parents that her ambition is for real...

Will Chloe get to live her dream?

9780746061176

Rising Star

Chloe's made it into top talent academy Rockley Park, and she's desperate to perform in the school's Rising Stars concert – she's heard that talent scouts often turn up from the big record companies. But she's got one problem...she can't find her voice!

Will Chloe miss her Big Chance?

9780746061183

Secret Ambition

A TV crew is coming to Rockley Park school and model twins Pop 'n' Lolly are the star attraction. The talented twosome are used to doing everything together and they make the perfect double act. So Pop can't understand why Lolly seems so fed up.

Will Pop discover Lolly's secret before she ruins their glittering career?

9780746061206

Rivals!

Talented drummer Danny is in constant demand at Rockley Park. But Charlie, the other drummer in his year, is jealous of Danny's success. Tension mounts between the two rivals, so when they're forced to play together in the school concert sparks could fly!

Who will come out on top?

9780746061190

Tara's Triumph

Tara is following her dream of becoming a rock star at Rockley Park. And when she hears about an African school for orphans, she decides that a charity CD would be a great way to raise money to help them.

Will Tara succeed or will she get herself into more trouble than she bargained for?

9780746068359

Lucky Break

Marmalade is one of the best dancers at Rockley Park. But he's also the class clown, and things get out of hand when a new boy arrives and Marmalade starts to show off even more than usual. It looks as though he's heading for a fall – literally!

Could this really be Marmalade's lucky break?

9780746068366

Solo Star

Chloe's thrilled when she hears she's been chosen to appear in the Rising Stars concert – the show is going to be on TV and this could be her big break! The only trouble is she has to perform with a band, when she's always wanted to be a solo star.

Will Chloe be able to shine onstage?

9780746073032

Christmas Stars

Rockley Park is buzzing with festive fun. Chloe and her friends are rehearsing for the Christmas concert and they've planned a secret surprise for their favourite teacher, Judge Jim. But then there's some shocking news, and it seems he won't make the concert after all.

Can everyone pull together to make Judge Jim's Christmas really sparkle?

9780746077429

Pop Diva

Twins Pop 'n' Lolly are already top models and now they've won a recording contract too. But Pop dreams of being a TV presenter and throws herself into this new obsession instead of concentrating on her singing. So when the girls get to record their new single, Pop's just not good enough.

Can Pop save her sparkling singing career?

9780746073049

Battle of the Bands

Chloe's band has won a prized place in an international Battle of the Bands competition. Every little detail has to be absolutely perfect for their performance, as it will be shown on TV around the world. So when Chloe's show-stopping dress is lost, it's a complete disaster!

Do they still stand a chance of winning the Battle of the Bands?

9780746078839

Star Maker

Since taking part in the Battle of the Bands, Tara's become a star at Rockley Park – and across the country too! Her band is set to play on TV and at a massive charity gig. But Charlie is jealous of her success and he's making Tara's life unbearable. The trouble is, when the band's drummer falls ill, Charlie is asked to play instead.

Can Tara stop feeling angry with Charlie and get the band through their biggest concert ever?

9780746097151

✳ All priced at £4.99 ✳

Cindy Jefferies' varied career has included being a Venetian-mask maker and a video DJ. Cindy decided to write *Fame School* after experiencing the ups and downs of her children, who have all been involved in the music business. Her insight into the lives of wannabe pop stars and her own musical background means that Cindy knows how exciting and demanding the quest for fame and fortune can be.

Cindy lives on a farm in Gloucestershire, where the animal noises, roaring tractors and rehearsals of Stitch, her son's indie-rock band, all help her write!

To find out more about Cindy Jefferies, visit her website: www.cindyjefferies.co.uk